God H .

Dr. Rev. Greg Hibbins

ISBN: 978-1-9164868-0-5
Caracal Publishing, United Kingdom

Preface

I'm really glad that you are reading this book, as I share with you the remarkable journey that God has taken me on. I share this testimony, which is a testimony of God's goodness. It is a testimony of the reality of a loving God who cares for His people and His creation, and how He came and intervened in my life as a young man—a young man completely opposed to God in every way and every form. Despite my opposition, He broke through to me, and I would like to share that journey—and things that he used to be to reach me—with you.

As we start, let's look at God's Word. 1 Peter 5:8 says, "Be sober minded, be alert, your adversary the devil is prowling around like a roaring lion, seeking for anyone he can devour."

We are living in a day and age where people don't believe in the reality of Satan; we are living in a day and age where people think it's all some sort of big joke. Entertainment, horror, fortune-telling and the huge panorama of related activities are designed to draw people deeper into Satan's snare and blind them to God. I pray my testimony will remind you that there is a Saviour, and His name is Jesus—and He came to save us.

Chapter 1: Early Years

I was born into an occultic home on the 27 July, 1959. My family was living in Durban, South Africa at that time. My mom was at home in labour with me; in those days not everybody went to the hospital to have a baby. The doctor and midwife were in with her. While she was in labour, the telephone rang and my granny who lived with us answered the telephone. It was the leader of the local spiritism sanctuary, and he said to my gran, "I just want to congratulate Jean on the birth of her baby son."

My Gran was quite puzzled and said, "Well, the baby has not been born yet, and we don't know the sex of the baby; so how can you call up to tell me to congratulate her on the birth of her baby son?"

As she said those words, she heard my cry come from the bedroom. He answered and said, "Just pass on the message to Jean."

You see, he knew what my gender was, and he knew the exact moment of my birth, even though he wasn't there. Those were the sort of incidents that took place which cemented in my mom's mind the power that was available in the occult. I was also born with the membrane over my face which, within many occult groups, is considered a sign of second sight and occultic ability. It was seen as a badge of approval, and literally from the day of my birth I was set aside by my mother and started to be trained in the occult.

Although I was born in Durban, South Africa, we moved up to Northern Rhodesia, now called Zambia, when I was six weeks old.

The relationship between my mom and dad was one which was full of tension and conflict. For both of them, it was a second marriage. I had a half-brother and a half-sister, 13 and 11 years older than me respectively, and a full brother who was three years older than me. The relationship between my mom and dad continued to disintegrate to the point that, when I was four, they decided to get divorced.

They were both professional people, and I grew up in a very wealthy home. I never wanted for anything materially, but it was a home devoid of affection and love. I have no recollection of us ever sitting down to a meal together, or of my mother or father showing any affection to each other or to me as a child. I remember my half-sister leaving at that time to get married and my half-brother leaving to join the South African Navy.

I remember very clearly before the final divorce hearing and custody ruling that my parents put me in an impossible situation. In those days it was normal for the children to be asked by the judge who they would like to go and live with. I remember very clearly my dad offering to buy me a pellet gun if I said him, and my mom offering to give me a little live animal called a bush baby if I would say her. You can imagine the turmoil I faced, as a four-year-old boy who loved both his mommy and his daddy being asked to make those sorts of decisions. I couldn't. When the judge asked me who I would prefer to live with, I could not give him an answer, because really, I felt I was being torn apart inside.

As was the norm in those days, the judge awarded custody to my mother, and for the next two years there was increased conflict between my parents. My dad had private detectives following my mom all the time; as soon as she did something that he felt he could use to try to get custody of us, he would go back to court and apply for temporary custody of us while the matter was investigated. For two years my brother and I were the pawns in their pitched battle for control — backwards and forwards, backwards and forwards between our parents' homes. It was an incredibly unsettling time, and even today, many years later, my heart breaks for the children of parents who are splitting up.

Through this whole time, my mom was continuing to disciple me in the occult. Also, the aggression, hate and anger that she felt towards my father was beginning to influence me negatively, and my relationship with my father suffered. At the age of six, she moved us back to South Africa for a few years, hoping that the distance would prevent my dad from having private detectives following her, and that the whole custody battle would just go away.

Chapter 2: Growing-Up

We had been in South Africa less than six months when my mother remarried again. That relationship didn't last very long and ended in another divorce. Throughout my formative years, there was almost a constant stream of men in and out of my mom's life, escalating as she became more and more involved in the occult and, as a result, their ceremonies and practices.

My dad would visit us in school holidays and take us with him for a week or two. During these times, we would go on hunting trips, fishing trips or beach holidays.

One such visit sticks very clearly in my mind. It happened soon after the divorce. My dad came to visit and took my brother and I to Durban for a two-week holiday where we stayed in an upmarket hotel on the beachfront. In the whole two weeks, my dad only ever took me out once; the rest of the time I stayed alone in the hotel suite while he and my brother went to the beach and other places. I consoled myself by ordering puff pastries filled with creamed mushrooms from room service. To this day I have no idea why I was excluded — I was not a naughty child — but that experience left a deep scar of loneliness and hurt in my life. It could have been that my dad could not cope with both my brother, who had learning difficulties, and me together — or perhaps it was his way of trying to hurt my mother, knowing of her interest in me as an occultic protégé.

Me (at 4 years old) with my brother

At the age of nine, my mom and dad decided to get remarried purely for practical purposes. My mom, I think, was exhausted by the fact that my dad was continuing to have private detectives following her and that he had the resources to do so indefinitely. I think she also realized that he wasn't going to let up until he had access to us boys. So, they got remarried, and we moved to what was then Southern Rhodesia (now Zimbabwe), to Salisbury and the suburb of Marlborough, to set up home.

We had a very big house; my mom had her wing, my dad his wing, and they would occasionally meet in the middle for all-out war.

My dad now had greater access to us, but the years apart had taken their toll on our relationship. Through the years, my mother had continued to pour out her hatred and anger into my easily-influenced young ears, so that by the time they remarried I had built up a huge amount of anger and savage aggression to my father, leading to a huge chasm of unforgiveness between us—a state of affairs that would last until his last six months of life.

One incident that sticks in my mind was when I was 14 and I returned home to find them arguing in the dining room. I was a very fit and strong young man by then and a brown belt in karate. I remember walking into the room and going straight up to my dad and hitting him in the side. He collapsed onto the floor and had difficulties breathing; he was taken to hospital where they diagnosed a broken rib. What we did not know at that time was that the cancer that would kill him within a year was already well established in his body.

It was from the age of nine, once we moved back up to Rhodesia, that my mom really started to intensify my occult training. There was a man who led the local occult movement, and I was apprenticed to him as his disciple. That's where my training really began in earnest. It involved everything from reading all the different occultic scripts for the various branches, modern literature that promoted the occult, meditation, levitation, spells, and many more things.

All of these occultic practices became part and parcel of my normal life. Spiritual guides would appear to me throughout the day and night, and we would have long and deep thought-provoking discussions. The two primary so-called guides were Native American and Chinese. Today, I realize that they were actually demons.

In addition, I remember the junior school did a bank of IQ tests, after which they called my parents to report that I was a gifted child and incredibly intelligent. The tests also already showed an emotional maturity of a young adult, even though I was only 11 at the time. My mother and mentor attributed these results to my long and detailed conversations with my spirit guides.

My peers at school were very scared of me. I would just look at them, feel my brow begin to tingle as I focused on them, and they would be very scared, often describing the sensation of feeling like millions of spiders were crawling over them. No one messed with me at school, and it is often this promise of occultic power that draws so many young people in.

At the age of 15, my dad passed away from cancer, but an incident six months before he died saw our relationship restored.

My dad had served in the Royal Navy in the Second World War. He served on destroyers and was on HMS Sikh, when it was sunk at

Tobruk; he spent 18 months as a POW, and it was during this time that he developed an ulcer that would turn to cancer in later life.

I remember arriving home one day from Sea Cadets. (I was part of T. S. Mashona, which was based at the Army Drill Hall in Salisbury.) This day, I had just been promoted to Leading Seaman. I remember walking into my dad's room; he was already in advanced stages of cancer, six months away from his death. I remember taking that red anchor — which was the badge of authority and the rank I had been given — and throwing it on his bed with these words, "You are probably not interested, but I was made Leading Seaman tonight."

As I said those words, I saw the tears well up in my dad's eyes and roll down his cheeks. Suddenly, for the first time, I realized that my dad actually did love me. I had allowed all the anger and hatred my mom had for my dad, together with all the things that happened and the constant input from the occultic forces, to build up a wall between me and my dad.

My dad was never involved in the occult. He would be what you call a good Church of England member; by that I mean that he would go on Christmas Day, Easter Sunday and maybe another one or two Sundays in the year. I was never allowed to go with him; my mom forbid it. I was never allowed even to have any contact with anybody who had anything to do with the

Bible or God. At school, my mother had arranged that when religious education was taking place I would go sit up in the library. I was not allowed to go to a church, go near a church, or discuss God or Jesus. In my world God and Jesus were swear words. So, I really knew absolutely nothing about Jesus Christ, I knew nothing about God, and I knew everything about Satan and the occultic ways.

Those last six months before my dad died brought an absolute breakthrough in our relationship. I grew very close to him. I carried him through to the bath and took over much of the personal care for him when I was home. Just after I turned 15, he died, and that year between 15 and 16 was quite a tumultuous year for me.

By the age of 15, I was really a fully-fledged spiritus medium. I was having my own séances on Wednesday night, to which people aged between 18 and 70+ came. Because I had already been picked out as one of the chosen, the occult leadership had already decided that I would join the South African Navy and rise very quickly in rank to get to positions where I would be able to influence people for Satan. An admiral from the SA Navy had flown up to Rhodesia to interview me for the Naval Academy. He was involved in the occult, and he was going to be my mentor once I moved into the Navy.

We need to realize that it tells us in Ephesians 6:12 that "we wrestle not against flesh and blood, but against principalities and powers, for our struggle is not against flesh and blood, but against the rulers against the authorities, against the cosmic powers of this darkness, against evil spiritual forces in the high places in the heavenlies."

What people don't realize is that the real, powerful Satanist is not the person who walks down the road dressed all in black. The real powerful Satanists are men and women who are sitting in high positions of authority — they are in the military, they are in the police force, they in the judicial system, they are in business, they are in government — and you would walk past them never realizing that these people are involved in the occult. But they are influencers. Many of them are wealthy people that are involved in every single level of society, and they have in place a system where the older occultists are preparing the younger ones, who will replace them. So, there is this constant feeding in of men and women into positions of power, influence and authority who have already given their allegiance to Satan. This was their plan for my life — a progression plan that they had mapped out for me in the SA Navy. I did not know it at the time, but God had another plan.

Just before my 16th birthday, the man who was my spiritus mentor said, "I'll be at your séance tonight; tonight you are to progress to higher things". In the séances I would go into a trance, different so-called spirits would possess me, and different voices would speak out through me and give messages to people about all sorts of things. My mentor highlighted again before the séance began that night that it was to be a special night. He said, "You are now ready to be initiated into the deeper things."

What I did not realize at that time was that he really meant that it was the night that I was to be fully demon possessed. As we began the séance, sitting on chairs in a circle, everything seemed the same as it had been many times before. But that night was to be different.

Please bear in mind that at up until that point I knew absolutely nothing about God—I had never read the Bible, I knew none of the Bible stories, I had not been involved in any way or form with any type of Christianity, or heard any Christian message. Over the years I've thought back to that night and what unfolded and asked myself, "Was there ever a time when I was exposed to Christianity, some situation or event that laid a seed in my mind as to who to call for help?"

The only vague memory that comes to mind is when I was about six years old; somebody was looking after me for the night (I think her name was Brenda and that she worked with my mother). I remember her taking me and my brother to a big tent; I remember that there was sawdust on the ground, a lot of singing, and a man at the front shouting a lot. My mother was very upset with the lady looking after us when she heard we had been taken to this place. I can only surmise that maybe it was one of the Gospel Tent Meetings that were held in the local towns. That's possibly the only time that I had ever heard the Gospel.

Now, as I sat in the séance and started to go into the trance, like I had many times before, a feeling of dread came over me and something inside my head said, "Don't do it!"

I felt only an absolute feeling of fear and dread and began to fight this force that was seeking to take me over, this supernatural being that was finally seeking to possess me. I started to fight it with all I had.

Now, I was a very fit, strong, young man. I had my age group national colours for sculling/rowing in the coxless fours, I played provincial cricket for my age group, I had fenced for years with both foil and epee. I had a brown belt in karate and had been shooting from the age of three. Despite how fit and strong I was, after about 15-20 minutes I was getting to the point of complete exhaustion; this force was bending my head and neck back over the chair. It had pushed my head so far back that I felt there was somebody behind me trying to snap my neck. My shoulders had been pulled around towards the back of the chair, and I felt like there was somebody with supernatural strength trying to split me apart down the middle. I just fought and fought and fought as much as I could.

While this was happening the 12-15 people sitting in the séance saw what was happening to me, yet not one of them stepped forward to assist or help me. My spiritus mentor was sitting there and he did nothing.

Eventually after nearly half an hour (I was told the duration later by others in the séance), I had reached exhaustion point, and I could just feel that these forces were overwhelming me. At that point, from somewhere, I just shouted out the words, "God, help me!"

As I shouted out those words, the forces that were holding onto me instantly let go. As they released me, I collapsed onto the floor, off my chair, and lay on the floor exhausted and gasping for breath. My spiritus mentor was fuming with anger; he grabbed hold of me by the shoulders and started bashing my head on the floor, screaming at me, "Why did you do that? Why did you do that? This was supposed to be the night that you would move into deeper things. Why did you do that?"

I could not answer him. I had no breath to speak and was too exhausted to even begin to fully comprehend what had taken place. My mentor stormed out, and that was the last time I saw him before other events began to unfold in my life.

That whole episode in the séance, paired

with my mentor's and mother's reactions—she too was furious with me—left huge question marks in my mind.

You see, my whole life I had been told that this was the way, this was the right thing, this was the plan for you. But at the same time, between the ages of nine and thirteen, I'd been subjected to satanic cultic meetings. In these meetings some very unpleasant things had happened to me.

I remember the first meeting I was taken to at age nine. It was in an evening, and the meeting was in a large barn; the floors were slate with a large pentagram engraved in the slate. In the middle of the barn was a huge black marble table which served as the altar. There must have been thirty to forty adults there, all dressed in black and red capes, with cowl hoods covering their faces. They were naked underneath the capes.

I was told to drink a milky liquid with a slightly bitter taste. After drinking the liquid, I entered a conscious but dreamy state and was very compliant to any instructions given. What happened after that and many other times at these gatherings would today be classed as SRA (Satanic Ritual Abuse). I have never spoken openly about what happened in those meetings as the memories are painful, especially as my own mother was an active participant in what was done to me.

Now, huge questions arose in my mind as I grappled with what had happened and the shaking of what, up until then, had been my whole worldview. Also bear in mind that I had never ever been to church — and even at that point had no desire or plan to have anything to do with God or His church in any way.

Chapter 3: Rush Hour Evangelism

The incident in the séance took place just before my 16th birthday. In Rhodesia, as it was then, you could get your driver's license at 16 years old. I could drive already, having driven on farms from the age of 12, but knew I would need to attend a driving school to learn the finer points needed to pass my test the first time. As a young guy — and you know what young guys are like — I had a lot of pride, a big ego. I knew I had to pass my test first time, which meant a driving school to master the finer points.

I get very excited when I get to this part of my testimony, because God used a strange method to get me to book at the particular driving school He wanted me to go to!

Just before I booked for my driving lessons, I had been to the movies and watched *Herbie Rides Again*. You may remember the Herbie movies about the little talking VW, whose number was 53. I loved the Herbie movies as a young man, and I really loved the VW Beatle. So, I decided I wanted to learn to drive in a VW Beatle. I looked around and did a little bit of research and found out there was only one driving school in the whole of Salisbury that used VWs. It was the Perioli Driving School. So, I phoned up and booked my appointments.

Their normal practice was to pick up the students in Cecil Square, Salisbury, Rhodesia, opposite the flower sellers. I duly arrived at a quarter to five for my lesson. There were two VW Beatles parked there, both with youngish women sitting in them. One of the women climbed out of the Beatle and approached me; she was in her early thirties. She asked if I was Greg, and when I replied in the affirmative, she identified herself as my driving instructor and said her name was Jenny.

Now, I must be honest, I was shocked! The last thing I had expected was a lady driving instructor. Like most young men of my age, I was a bit egotistic and macho, and the thought of a lady taking me for driving lessons filled me with horror. Jenny saw my confusion, gave a knowing smile, and told me to get in the car. I found out later that Jenny had been a policewoman and patrol car driver and was more than qualified for the job.

Once in the car, she asked me if I had done any driving. When I told her I had and explained that I had driven on friends' farms for years, Jenny instructed me to start the car and pull out into the traffic. However, there was one small problem. It was 5pm! All the shops had just closed, and everyone was heading home for a swim and a cold cooldrink. In Salisbury in October, the temperature would soar; it was called 'Suicide Month' as the extremely hot weather seemed to escalate the suicide rate.

Into this rush-hour traffic of hot, tired and frustrated drivers, this unsuspecting learner was thrust. I had never driven in the city, I had never driven in traffic, and I had certainly never realized that there were so many angry drivers on the road, all of whom seemed to be honking their horns at me. I was terrified! Jenny on the other hand was as calm as a cucumber, seemingly having nerves of steel and no fear for her life.

All Jenny seem interested in doing was talking to me about this guy called Jesus and how much He loved me and that I needed Him in my life. After about 15 minutes and a scary number of near collisions, I was a wreck. I blurted out, "Please stop talking about this Jesus guy! Can we concentrate on my driving? After all, that's what I am paying for."

I must give Jenny her due; she had a cast-iron means of evangelizing. She had me right where she wanted me, desperate and terrified for my life in the midst of this sea of angry drivers.

"Ok," she said, "But only if you agree to come to church with me on Friday night. I'll even let you drive there."

That was enough for me. I was desperate, so I agreed to go with her—and from that point on we focused on my driving, and I survived my first lesson.

True to her word, Jenny arrived on Friday evening at my house to pick me up. I had not told my mother where I was going, only that my driving instructor was taking me for a night driving lesson. I took the wheel of the VW and off we went. Now, that VW was only a 6-volt model, which meant that the headlights were not very bright, and all my concentration was required just to see the road ahead as it was a very dark night. Jenny was very quiet, occasionally giving me pointers about driving at night. On reflection, I think she was praying for me.

We arrived at the Assemblies of God Church on McCleary Avenue about 10 minutes before the meetings began. The place was packed with young people and young adults. We walked in and I sat at the very back, oozing hostility and aggression; I was there under duress. The program started with a film called *The Other Side of the Mountain* and was followed by a young man getting up to preach.

The preacher's name was Bushy Venter, and in normal conversation he stuttered very badly. But when he got up to preach, the stutter disappeared!

That night, I heard for the first time the Gospel of Jesus Christ, and as Bushy preached I felt myself coming under deep conviction of sin, and a sense of desperation filled me. When Bushy gave an appeal and invited people to come forward and accept Christ as their Saviour, I exploded out of the back pew and was the first to reach the front. That night, the 10th of October, 1975, I gave my heart to Jesus and felt the physical and spiritual release of sin and the occultic bondage that had entrapped me. As we left the church, I could not stop crying tears of joy and release. Jenny drove me home, not saying much again, but outside my house she took my hand and prayed for me and welcomed me to God's family.

As I walked in my front door, my mother was standing in the living room area. She swung round with a look of utter hatred on her face and screamed at me, "What have you done?"

You see, as I walked into that house for the first time, the Spirit of God, which was now in me, walked in with me, and all the occultic forces of darkness reacted to the presence of God.

My mother was not happy that I had become a Christian, she was not happy that I'd been born again, and for the next week war broke out in our home — a spiritual war and a physical one. My mom did everything she could to try and get me to turn my back on Jesus Christ.

Every night when I fell asleep, my bedroom was invaded by demonic forces, this time not masquerading as the Native American or the Chinese man they had been when they were my spirit guides. But now I saw them for what they really were — horrific demons, unmasked and terrifying to see. Night after night, masses of these stinking, horrific beings would pack into my room, seeking to intimidate and force me to abandon Jesus. One night I awoke to feel the demonic hands on my throat, choking me; I could not breathe or speak, but just cried out in my mind, "Jesus, help me!"

Again, immediately as those words crossed my mind, the demonic forces left my room.

Eventually, after a week, my mother came to me and gave me an ultimatum, "Either lose Jesus, or you get out the house. If you don't lose Jesus, you lose your inheritance… and you will leave this home with nothing."

My dad, in the last six months of his life, had shown me his will, which he had lodged with his lawyers in the UK. In that will he had left everything, which was a significant amount, to me and my brother. His lawyer in the UK was to administer his estate. He had left nothing to my mother; they had been adversaries for much of their marriage and she also had her own resources.

My mother, however, had had another plan. She must have seen my dad's original will or been told about it by my brother who had also been there when Dad showed us the original will. A week before he died, my mom made a new will. By this time, my dad was already then in the advanced stages of cancer, high on the morphine he was prescribed and not really coherent anymore. My mom went into his room with the new will and came out with it signed by him and witnessed by her two friends. The new will had given her total control of everything.

My mother was a master manipulator and used her control over my dad's estate to try and intimidate me to reject Jesus. She reiterated to me again, that if I didn't lose Jesus Christ, then I would lose my inheritance. She thought that would be the incentive that would bring me under her control.

I caught a bus into town, and I was walking through the streets of the city, saying, "God, what must I do?"

I was a new Christian. I didn't know the Bible, and I hardly knew anything about Jesus. But the one thing I did know was Jesus Christ and the reality of that meeting. The reality of my salvation had impacted me, and I knew there was no going back to my old life.

Chapter 4: Army

I found myself walking down Union Avenue in Salisbury, and as I looked up, there in front of me was the Army recruitment office. Suddenly, it just felt like a window had opened. The army was somewhere I could go, so I walked in and told the recruitment sergeant that I wanted to volunteer for my national service.

At that time, Rhodesia was involved in a bush war, and at 18 you were called up for national service. Once you completed national service, you then were called up through the years as a territorial soldier. The army was desperately short of men. The recruiter was amazed when he found out I was only 16 and said I would need my parents' permission to enlist as a boy soldier.

I filled in the forms and took them up to the firm where my mother worked in finance. It was a major stationers that covered three floors. I rode the escalator up to her office and walked in and said, "You want to get rid of my Jesus; you want to get rid of me. Sign these forms, and we are out of your life."

After a glance at the forms, she signed, and I walked out of her life. I went back into the recruitment office, turned in the signed forms, and the process was put into play. I moved out of my home, stayed with a friend's family as I finished off my last school exam, and within a week—after passing my medical—found myself assigned to basic training in the RLI (Rhodesian Light Infantry) commandos.

Army basic training was a wake-up call! I was a young man who, although fairly disciplined within myself, had never experienced a lot of discipline growing up in my home.

Growing up, I wanted for nothing in terms of possessions; there was always money, and money was often used as a replacement for attention. There were always possessions, but no real affection. There wasn't any real family life. As mentioned, I have no recollection of us ever sitting down to eat a meal together. I would ring a little bell; the cook would come and take my order and then bring the food to where I wanted to eat it.

My relationship with my brother had been quite a fractious one; he was three years older than me and used to bully me. At the age of 13 and having done martial arts for a number of years, I took him on and sorted him out. After that, he left me alone and never tried to bully me again.

So, basic training was a huge wake-up call for me. RLI was a place where character was formed. It was a steep learning curve, but in Barrack Room Sable, on the third floor of training troop, I grew closer to God. The church had given me a little *Living Bible*, and I devoured it. I spent what little free time we had reading it and sharing my newfound faith with my fellow recruits.

I grew to greatly respect our training troop CSM (Company Sergeant Major), Moose Erasmus. He was a hard but fair man who pushed us to the limits and beyond — and transformed us into men.

Going into the army I was already fairly well trained in the skills of drill, having been a Sea Cadet and having led a drill squad of my own. Also, because my dad had been a gun enthusiast and collector, together with being a reserve police inspector, I was familiar with most of the weapons we used and could already strip down the weapons. I had been shooting since the age of three and was already a sniper-grade marksman. Tracking was another skill I took into the army with me; I had been taught by my father's Bushman tracker during our numerous hunting trips.

Already having these skills allowed me to thrive during basic training. It was something I actually enjoyed, as we were formed into useful soldiers. After three months of basic training and with the Bush War escalating, we passed out of training and were assigned to our commandos. Under normal circumstances, they would not have sent boy soldiers up to the front, but the need for trained soldiers was great, and a number of us who were not far off our 17th birthdays were deployed along with the rest of the commando. Support Commando deployed up to the NE

Border into the Operation Hurricane area.

On the first day of our deployment, one of our vehicles hit a landmine and we suffered our first casualty. This was not a game but real war, where real men died and were wounded. It was a sobering time, and we all focused on the task at hand.

During basics I had befriended a young Afrikaans guy called Johan and had led him to Jesus six weeks before we deployed. Our stick was deployed on patrol in an area with a suspected terrorist presence. We were a couple hours into the patrol when we had contact with the enemy. Suddenly, there were bullets flying everywhere, and we took cover.

Our corporal, the NCO, took a moment to access the situation, but in the commando, you did not take cover for too long, you assessed and then you moved forward. I remember the call came, and we started to move forward using the strategies we had trained in. We were moving forward, leapfrogging each other and double tapping (firing two shots in your firing arc in front of you). I was moving forward and double tapped in front of a bush, and suddenly this terrorist reared up from behind it; my bullets had flushed him out. Training takes over at that point, and as I dived for cover, I double tapped just as he too opened fire on us.

The next thing I remember was lying on the ground, but my two bullets had hit the terrorist in the chest — one in the breastbone and the other in his heart. There was no time to process what had just happened; we were in the middle of a firefight, you just moved on.

Eventually, when it was all over and the helicopters were coming into collect bodies and pick us up, I remember looking down at the body of the man I had shot and asking the Lord, "I'm not even 17 years old yet, but I've taken a life?" All these thoughts were running through my mind, and I wondered, *Lord, what happening?* I felt really sick.

We went back to base and the next day deployed, and that cycle repeated itself. Five weeks into that cycle of deployment, while part of 'Fire Force' (helicopter-borne troops dropped into contact situations), we were again in a contact with the enemy.

Once again, we were leapfrogging forward. My friend Johan, who I had led to the Lord during basic training, was about 5 or 6 meters in front of me and to my left. As I started to move forward to leapfrog him, he was hit directly in the chest by an RPG rocket. I was blown off my feet, but his body had absorbed most of the blast and that is what probably saved my life. I was shattered by Johan's death, and I was really battling mentally to deal with all that I had seen and experienced.

We finished that six-week deployment and headed back to our barracks in Salisbury. At that stage, we spent six weeks in the bush and eight days out. There was normally a day's travel on either side, which meant we really only had six days of R&R (rest and recuperation).

I was renting a little garden flat in the avenues area of Salisbury and returned home. We had cleared barracks on the Friday, and I was determined to go to the young adults group at church that night, as I knew I needed help to process all that had taken place. I drove out to church and entered the hall where we were meeting. I approached the two men who led the group and asked them if I could speak to them straight after the meeting. I informed them that I had just returned from a bush trip and needed help to process some of the things that had happened.

The young adults group was about 100 strong, and 80% of the people there were attractive young women. After the meeting I stood waiting, but the two leaders were busy chatting up the girls and appeared to have forgotten my request. After waiting a long time, my patience ran out. I smashed my coffee cup down and walked out of the church and drove home, very disappointed. I felt let down by the leaders.

The next morning, I phoned the church and tried to book an appointment to speak to one of the two pastors. I was told that they would not be available for the rest of the next week. After asking further questions, I discovered that they were involved in a pastors' golf week. I never play golf, and to this day I have a mental block against the game. After 40 years of ministry, I have seen too many ministers playing golf and not spending enough time caring for their flocks.

I put the phone down. I had had enough of Christians! I had had enough of church! From that point on, I turned my back on God. I started to run from God, and for the next two years, I headed off down my own path. The things that happened in those years would fill another book, but the reality was that I was running from God.

Six months later, while back on 6 days R&R, I was sitting on my verandah, cleaning my rifle and bush kit. I heard my gate open, and as I looked up, I saw the two youth leaders from church walk in — the same two who had been too busy chatting up the girls to speak to me. They greeted me and started to tell me how much they had missed me. I was having none of their hypocrisy; I reached down, picked up a magazine of bullets (we called them rounds), and clipped it into my rifle. I then cocked my rifle to chamber a round and said to them, "I don't need you or your God; if you are not out of that gate by the time I count to five, I'm going to start shooting." They ran for their lives.

All they had shown me was a very shallow Christianity, but I did not realize it at that time, I was still looking to people, not God.

The one constant in those days was that every time I deployed into the bush, I had my little Gideon Bible in my backpack. I never read it, but it was there.

I finished my year of volunteer national service and was given the choice to sign up as an army regular. I really enjoyed the army, but after much thought, declined. I think I knew even then that the odds were stacked against the brave country that was Rhodesia, and my thoughts went to what would be best for my future.

Me, just after completing National Service
(I'm sitting on my hands,
because the car was hot and burning my legs.)

Chapter Five: Training

As mentioned previously, I was considered gifted, with an academic IQ of 154, but due to the circumstances that had led me to leave home early, I had neither the money, nor the M or A levels required for university.

However, I needed to earn a living to pay rent and feed myself. A conversation I had had with my Dad before his death popped into my mind. I remembered him saying that a person with a trade behind them should never be without work and that they could travel the world. I liked fast cars and decided that perhaps a trade as a motor mechanic/technician would be good. There was a challenge though. Most of the apprenticeship openings had been advertised in July and August while I was still in the army. However, I like to meet problems and challenges head on, so I set off for the biggest motor dealership we had in Salisbury — Cairns Motors. I walked into their main branch on Union Avenue and asked to see their training manager, Phil Hards.

I was shown into Phil's office, and he asked me what he could help me with. When I replied that I was looking for an apprenticeship, he smiled and shook his head. "All the openings have already been filled; why did you not apply earlier?" he asked me.

"Well Sir," I replied. "I was in the bush

doing my National Service."

Mr Hards' eyes narrowed, and a speculative look came over his face. "What school did you go to?"

"Allan Wilson, Sir." I replied.

Mr Hards smiled. Allan Wilson was a high school that you had to pass a high standard entrance test to attend; students there did the normal academic subjects but also did additional technical subjects. They had produced a lot of engineers and professional people.

"When can you start?" he asked.

A bit surprised, I replied, "On Monday, Sir. But why the opening if they are filled?"

Once again, he smiled and explained. It turned out that all the newly-engaged apprentices had been called up by the army to do their National Service, and the duration had just been raised that very week from 1 year to 2 years. This meant that the company would not see their apprentices for two years but would still be responsible to give them 'make-up pay' (the difference between their army pay and apprenticeship pay). Because I had completed my National Service, I would be called up as a territorial soldier on a 'six weeks in, six weeks out' basis, and therefore the company would get some use out of me. I was ecstatic, and deep down I knew that even though I was running from God, His lovingkindness was still going before me.

I started my 'appyship,' but within a few weeks was called up as a territorial soldier. I was a sergeant by then, just seventeen and a half years old. My special skills of sniper and tracker were in short supply, and those who had them 'enjoyed' a high call-up ratio. After three, six-week call-ups with 'F' Company, 1RR (1st Battalion Rhodesian Regiment), based at the Drill Hall on Moffatt Street, I decided to try out for Special Forces as I felt they would be more my fit. I joined Special Forces (Selous Scouts) as a territorial member with the TA Support Group (their name was later changed to Assault Group) in mid-1979.

The 'six weeks in, six weeks out' call-up cycle was proving challenging as it did not fit the cycle of technical training my employer needed me to attend at the Polytechnic. My employer, Cairns Motors, and the army came to an agreement that would work for both. It was decided that my call-ups would be 3- to 4-month blocks, followed by a block of Polytechnic or practical 'on the bench' time at work.

Because of my position of being able to do long blocks of call-up as opposed to most other TAs who were on the 6-week cycles, I was attached to 1 Group, which was based at Rusape. Our forward camps were called forts. Fort Rusape was alongside a dirt airstrip, and our OC (Officer Commanding) was Maj. C.W. Donald, nicknamed Chipper.

Me in Special Forces

Chapter Six: Wake-Up Call

It was on one of these call-ups in late 1978 that God decided He had had enough of my running from Him.

As Special Forces, we were operating in a 'frozen area' — an area were no other security forces were allowed to venture or operate, because special forces were often doing recon work dressed as the enemy. We had been there for two weeks and had received no information at all; we called that a 'lemon' as the mission has soured. I was with one other Special Force soldier and 3 auxiliaries or TTs (Tame Terrs) — enemy combatants who had been captured and had agreed to work with us. I radioed our Major, and he agreed that it was time to 'uplift' us (pick us up).

Special Forces mostly deployed, or were uplifted, at night. This avoided us being compromised. We had agreed that the pick-up point would be at Watsomba, a small local business trading area 42kms north of Umtali, on the Umtali-Inyanga road. In those days, it was really just a piece of bare ground with some thatched umbrellas under which the locals sat and sold their wares. Two trucks had been dispatched from our base in Rusape, a driver and two escorts per truck. We were in hiding on a small hill close to the road when I saw the vehicles' lights in the distance. I radioed the convoy commander and said we would put our packs in the middle of the road, so he knew where to stop.

There was a full moon that night, and as we walked into the clear, open ground of the business centre, all 'hell' broke loose. There were 130 terrorists waiting in ambush for us—100 on my side of the road and another 30 on the other side—and they had us in a crossfire. A tremendous wall of gunfire came towards us, and I remember as I saw that wall of tracer fire while falling to take cover on the ground, that these words flashed through my mind, *God, I don't want to die tonight.*

What happened next was amazing! For the first time in my life I heard God speak to me very clearly and audibly—and there was no doubt in my mind that this was the voice of God. He said, "You have a choice to make. You serve me for the rest of your life, or I will take you home tonight."

And I said, "Lord, I'm going to serve you."

I heard God's voice, and I recognized it for Who He was. There is no mistaking His voice when He speaks.

As we hit the ground, I glanced back, and the three auxiliaries had disappeared back into the bush. We later suspected one of them had compromised us and given up information to the enemy. My other soldier was lying to my right and just behind me; his head was level with my bush boots (veldskoene).

Both of use were returning fire, and as the first vehicle arrived in the ambush area, it was hit by an RPG rocket, right in the front by the engine. The guys inside were okay, as they were protected by heavy armour plating. The second vehicle was also hit by heavy machine gun fire and immobilized.

We were out in the open, completely exposed, and clearly visible as it was full moon. The enemy was pouring down heavy machine gun fire on us, together with a mixture of rockets and a few mortars thrown in for good measure.

Suddenly, after half an hour, all their firing stopped simultaneously, and they ran away. I radioed the men in the trucks to check they were okay and also to identify ourselves as we did not want them to shoot us by mistake.

Due to the high mountains in the area, we needed to contact our base via a radio relay station which was on top of one of the highest mountains; it was called Oscar-Alpha 3, if I remember correctly. As I called the relay station, the operator came up on the air very excited, "01-Golf, did you see the fireworks? Someone has been in a big contact!"

They had seen the tracer fire from their high vantage point. Once I had calmed him down enough to follow instructions, I relayed a message to our OC in Rusape. Both of our vehicles were immobilized and could not be driven. Our OC arranged for RLI, who were based at Grand Reef, Umtali, to come and pick us up.

We returned to the scene at first light. It was quite a sight to see! The ground where we had been lying was heavily scarred by machine gun fire, as well as rocket and mortar blasts. But, the area where we had been lying was blast free, for a diameter of about sixteen feet. There was an almost perfect circle around were we had been lying, almost as if God had put a force field around us. One of our most experienced trackers came up to me and said, "*Ishe* (which means sir), you should be dead, but God was with you." Never had a truer word been spoken.

I finished my call-up a week later, and after four heavy months in the bush, I needed to decompress. So, I took a month of leave from work and went to Durban, South Africa, for a holiday. It had been my normal practice to hit the discos when not on call-up—I had won a disco free style and rock and roll competition in my teen years—but things were different now.

I spent the time on holiday reading my Bible, praying and getting things right between me and God. I had blamed God for my failures and the church's failure to help me when I needed help, but the reality was that God had not failed me—people had. I learnt the valuable lesson that people will let you down, but God will not.

I flew back to Salisbury after my holiday, and as I walked into my front door, the phone was ringing. I answered, and a girl I had not seen for a number of years was on the line; her name was Trish. She said, "Greg, where have you been? I've been ringing the whole week and getting no answer."

I could hear the exasperation in her voice, but I was a bit wary of Trish; the last time I had heard from her had been 18 months before. Then she had phoned to ask to borrow my car to run an urgent errand for her dad who was a farmer. I had lent her my car which she promptly written off in an accident two hours later. My eyes drifted to the window, through which I could see my beloved new *Alpha* sports car.

"Why have you been trying to reach me, Trish?" I asked, hoping she did not need to borrow my car again as that would be a firm no.

"This whole week in my prayer time, God has been bringing your face before me. I just had to try and contact you! What are you doing tonight?"

With a sigh of relief—my car was safe—I answered, "Nothing. Why?"

"Will you come to church with me tonight? My church, Salisbury Baptist, has a young adults group on a Friday night, and I think God wants you there," she blurted out.

"Sure, Trish. I will come, but I'll pick you up. I'm driving."

Trish could hear the laughter in my voice and quickly agreed. That night, I picked her up, and as per normal, she was running late getting ready, so by the time we arrived, the hall was filled with about 120 young adults. As I approached the door, the volume of noise rolling out was very loud; the young adults were doing a lot of talking and laughing. As I stepped through the doorway, all the talking died, and you could hear a pin drop. All eyes were looking at me — longish, wild hair; big bushy beard; and a big 38 Special revolver on my hip. I was not your normal patron of a church young adult group.

Then, a young man left the group and approached me; his name was Neil, and we had been at school together. "Is that you, Greg?" he asked, not sure if this wild man was the guy he knew from school. I laughed, and the tension was broken. The group settled down, and the meeting began soon after.

After the meeting on a Friday, all the young adults would go out for milkshakes at our local drive-in restaurant called *The Gremlin*. That night an incident took place that showed how much work God had to do in me. We had ordered and were sitting around our cars talking. Two of the girls had gone to the toilet in the main building; just as they started to return to where we were parked, the local 'Hell's Angels' motorcycle gang pulled in. They immediately started to circle the girls on their bikes, making rude comments to them. I responded in a flash, running up to their leader, pulling him off his bike, and jamming the barrel of my revolver in his mouth. I cocked the hammer back and said, "If your boys are not back out through the exit gate in 30 seconds, then your small brain is going to be splattered inside your fancy German helmet." On looking into my eyes, his 'boys' knew I meant it. Killing had become as natural as breathing to me, and I was very hard and callous. They fled, and he followed seconds later, as white as a sheet.

God had a lot of transforming work to do in me. I meet with the pastor of the church, told him my past, and I remember his response. His name was John Broom. John picked up his Bible and said, "Get to know this book. Allow the Holy Spirit to transform you. Feed on God's Word."

I have given that same advice to hundreds of people over the last forty years; it is still as true today as it was then. Romans 12:2 says, "Do not be conformed to this age, but be transformed by the renewing of your mind, so that you may discern what is the good, pleasing, and perfect will of God."

Chapter 7: A New Direction

As I grew in the Lord and in my involvement in the church, I felt God beginning to draw me towards full time ministry.

The war in Rhodesia was moving towards a political solution, and after talking to the Chaplain General, Lt. Colonel Norman Wood, he arranged my transfer from Selous Scouts on the 30th of January 1980 to the Chaplains Corp, were I served out my final call-up until April, 1980.

Rhodesia ceased to be in April, 1980, and became Zimbabwe. The majority of my final 3 months in the army was spent travelling from camp to camp, giving out Bibles and holding services. God was good, and a number of men came to know the Lord.

As 1980 sped by, I knew for sure that God wanted me in ministry. In September, I applied to do my trade test and passed, becoming a journeyman qualified automatic technician. That in itself was a miracle considering how little time I had actually spent at work due to call-ups.

I began to actively seek out God's will to see which seminary I should go to.

I had met Jerry Falwell Sr. on one of his trips to Rhodesia; he had asked about my life and I had shared my testimony with him. I was really surprised when 6 weeks after his return to the USA, I received a letter from him offering me a full three-year scholarship to Liberty University. In my mind, God had opened the door, but my pastor also encouraged me to apply to the Baptist Theological College of Southern Africa, the place where he had trained. I had my heart set on the USA, but to please John, I also applied to the Baptist College. To my amazement, they requested that I fly down for an interview at the college in Johannesburg.

Me just after the war ended

God does not always make it easy; sometimes you have to work hard to find His will. The night before I flew down to Johannesburg for my interview, I received a phone call from Pastor Stan Hannan at Mabelreign Chapel, another Baptist church. They had just had a meeting and decided to call me as their associate pastor; it would mean working at the church and studying by correspondence. All of a sudden, I had three possible avenues to follow.

I flew down to the Baptist College and upon arrival discovered that there were a number of students lined up for interviews that day. The interviews were with the full college council, a daunting prospect.

I was number three on the list, and as I sat in the waiting room, candidate number one went in. His interview lasted thirty-five minutes. In the meantime, I had struck up a conversation with candidate number four, Dawie, and he offered to drop me off at the station after his interview.

Candidate number two went in; his interview took forty-five minutes. Now, it was my turn. With a feeling of real trepidation, I stepped into the room to be confronted by a long table full of very serious looking people. They asked me three questions, and five minutes after my interview began, I found myself once more outside the room, interview over. Dawie's interview took fifty-five minutes, and as we travelled in his car to the station, I was convinced that I had been rejected.

We had to phone the registrar the next day for the decision on our admission. Once he answered and I identified myself, I asked him for the bad news. Mr Smart, the registrar just laughed, "No bad news," he said. "You were the quickest candidate through; we were all 100%

convinced that God has a call on your life and that you are meant to be at our seminary."

As I hung up the phone, I heard God speak again, "This is where I want You."

In January, 1981, I started at the Baptist Theological College of Southern Africa. Little did I know it then, but a beautiful, newly-qualified nurse from Rhodesia had just arrived at the Johannesburg General Hospital to do her midwifery qualification. The Johannesburg General was right opposite the seminary, and that nurse would one day be my wife. But that is another story, for another time.

Chapter 8: Reflections

As I look back over my early life and the war years I realize that:

- God always has a plan.
- We must look to God and not people. People will always let you down at some point; God will never let you down.
- Jesus never leaves us; we leave Him.
- God's ways are not our ways, but His ways are best.
- God's Word is true.
- Jesus is our healer — no matter who we are, no matter what we have done or had done to us. Jesus is able to bring full healing and restoration.
- God is real, and He loves you and me. But you have a choice: you can accept His free gift of salvation or reject it. The choice is yours.

Appendix 1: Documents from the day

Completion of apprenticeship

Note the remission granted because I had completed
National Service prior to starting my apprenticeship.

CERTIFICATE OF TERMINATION

(To be filled in on completion of the term of apprenticeship under this contract)

THIS IS TO CERTIFY THAT the within-named GREGORY STUART HIBBINS

.... has completed his apprenticeship under this

contract, this SECOND day of AUGUST 19. 80

CAIRNS MO....

Employer

TERMINATION NOTED.
REGISTRAR OF
APPRENTICESHIP
1980
....
SALISBURY, RHODESIA

.... 19......

Registrar of Apprenticeship

* "Granted a remission of 135 days from the indenture in terms of
section 38(3)(a) of the Apprenticeship Training and Skilled
Manpower Development Act, (Chapter 266) by virtue of undergoing
military training prior to entering into a Contract of
Apprenticeship. New termination date : 2nd August, 1980."

DATE : ....

SIGNED :
for REGISTRAR OF APPRENTICESHIP

Call-up notice to inform us of unit changes

TO: .... FROM:

Enter Name & Address or Addressograph Plate Here

Enter Unit Address & Date Stamp

MOBILISATION NOTICE

1. In terms of paragraph 5 of section 17 of the National Service Act, 1976, you are to report for service with this unit at the above address, no later than ___0400___ hours on ___24 11___ 19 _79_. Subject to the exigencies of the service, you will be stood down on ___26 11___ 19 _79_.

2. You will acknowledge receipt of this notice by completing the tear off portion below and returning it in the envelope in which this notice came, within 7 days, or disciplinary action will be taken.

3. Should you intend applying for a deferment or exemption, you should make immediate application to this unit for a deferment. Application for exemption should only be submitted to the Exemption Board once you have received this unit's comments. Exemption Boards will not entertain applications which have not been submitted properly.

4. If you are medically unfit, or should become unfit after you have returned the Acknowledgement of Mobilisation Notice, you are to IMMEDIATELY advise this unit in writing, together with the appropriate Doctor's Certificate. You will then be advised what further action to take.

5. Joining and other pertinent instructions are attached.

Note: Return address is overleaf · Tear off here

Letter from my OC after call-up to take back to employer

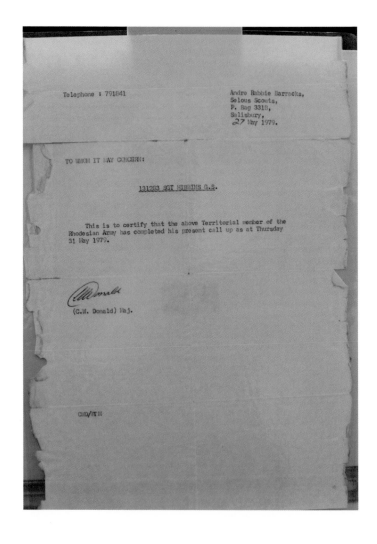

Telephone : 791841

Andre Rabbie Barracks,
Selous Scouts,
P. Bag 331B,
Salisbury,
27 May 1979.

TO WHOM IT MAY CONCERN:

131283 SGT HIGGINS G.S.

This is to certify that the above Territorial member of the Rhodesian Army has completed his present call up as at Thursday 31 May 1979.

(C.W. Donald) Maj.

CWD/ITM

Radio Issue Form

Printed by the Government Printer, Salisbury

ISSUE & RECEIPT VOUCHER

RA/Q/1031 (large—in books of 100)
Voucher must accompany stores if practicable

- Office stamp

- Consignor (original and triplicate)
  Consignee (duplicate)

Signature

	ISSUE voucher number and date	RECEIPT voucher number and date
	13/5/79	

Account	Account
Issued by	Issued to
Selous Scouts (Pварфе)	Sgt Hibbins
Authority for issue	Date and mode of conveyance

Sheet No.	No. of sheets	Invoice number and date

Ledger folio	VAOS or part number	Section or subsection DESIGNATION	Quantity	Description and marks on packages	For Store Depot use only				
					Line posting	Balance	Location	Rate	Value
(1)	(2)	(3)	(4)	(5)	(6)	(7)	(8)	(9)	(10)
		A63	1	97/08					$
		Telehand							
		Whip Antennae							
		Goose neck							
		Coax							
		Spul – mic.							
		Corde – weighted							

Military Driver's License

RHODESIA

Military Driver's Licence

Name S.G.T. HIBBINS · G.S

Military Motor Vehicle Driver's Licence

Granted by the Military Authorities

No. AL283 Date 2 February 1979

Regimental No. 131283

Rank Sgt

Name Hibbins G.S.

Unit Salmon mammba

is hereby licensed to drive a Gp B only

....

Licensing Officer.

DATE STAMP
- 2 FEB 1979
Bulawayo, Rhodesia

REMARKS AND ENDORSEMENTS

NOT Valid as a civilian drivers licence

Valid for duration of Military Service

Other Army Related Documents

Support Group,
Palace Barracks,
Auxa Nable Barracks,
P. Bag 331B,
Salisbury,
September 1979.

Telephone: 791841
Extension: \\\

TA Members
Support Group.

CALL UP INTERVIEWS - SUPPORT GROUP

1. It has become increasingly evident, since the formation of Support Group, that the Members of the Group are divided into two distinct categories. These are:

    a. Members who are more than willing to accept their responsibilities in respect to their Military commitments.

    b. Members who are Saturn Scouts in name only. That is to say they enjoy the reputation of being a member of the Unit but never do very little to any commitment to justify the wearing of the Brown Beret.

2. While the above statement might appear to be unjustified in respect of the average individual, it remains a fact in the case of certain members, and it is to these people that this directive is initially .....

3. It is appreciated, only too well, by the Commanding Officer, Lt Col Makin-coly, and Support Group that some members have very good reasons for requesting exemptions and deferments. It is also appreciated that all of you, with the odd exceptions, have "burnt your arse" to pass the Selection Course to gain entry into the Unit and also have stuck your necks out on numerous operations.

4. However, no Army Unit can hope to function when less than 50% of a call-up report for duty.

5. To this end the following policy will be implemented with immediate effect:

    a. All members who cannot carry out their call up when called upon to do so, will apply for an exemption from the Exception Board. N.b. No exceptions can or will be given by a member.

    b. Members will be given the opportunity to select their call up dates and where humanly possible, call ups will be within the period given by the individual. Members are responsible for notifying C Sgt Lewis (2i/C, Callup Office) of their call up preferences for the 1980 commitments by 1 December 1979.

    c. Those members who do not take the opportunity to nominate their call up periods will be allocated periods by this Unit in accordance with operational requirements.

/2. While ...

6. While it is not the policy of the Unit to remove members who cannot meet their commitments it has become imperative that if Support Group is to meet the tasks given to it by COMOPS, the Group must be in a position to know its operational strength per call up. To this end each individual must examine his personal position and if he cannot meet a minimum of 75% of his annual commitment he will be expected to request a posting to some other unit.

7. The case of individuals who feel they live in Sensitive areas and thereby warrant special treatment cannot be accepted as this is a Military Unit and has a job to carry out. Besides which the majority of this Country is classified as a Sensitive area.

COURSES

8. This has for a long time been a bone of contention amongst the TA members of the Unit and it will now be Support Group's policy to nominate 10% of every call up to attend a Specialist Course of some degree or other.

9. The Course members will be required to attend, will be:

    a. Demolitions (2 weeks).

    b. 106 Anti-tank Course (2 weeks).

    c. 81 and 60mm Mortar Course (2-3 weeks).

    d. Diving (Sub-aqua) (2 weeks).

    e. Watermanship (1 week).

    f. Free Fall (5 weeks).

    g. Snipers Course (3 weeks).

10. Those of you who have a desire to attend any of the courses mentioned are to indicate your preference in writing to C Sgt Lewis. Where there are limited nominations on courses preference will be given to the older members of the Unit.

GENERAL

11. a. It is hoped in the near future to institute a Quarterly Support Group Newsletter which will be sent to all members to keep them in the picture with the activities and movements of the Group and Unit. Anyone with any ideas or suggestions for the Newsletter are requested to forward them to the Group 2IC Capt Smith.

    b. The Osprey Pub is in the process of being renovated and with immediate effect all functions at the Support Group Pub will be open to wives, girlfriends, etc.

    c. The Group held a small informal farewell party for Capt and Mrs White on Saturday 8 September in the Osprey. Capt White was presented with a carved ivory tusk and Mrs White received a gold Osprey broach and a silver cigarette box. All items were suitably inscribed.

(R. Passaportis) Capt,
    OC Sp Gp,

RJAP/DAP

131283 Sgt., Hibbins G.S.
26, Ascot Road,
Avondale West,
SALISBURY.

Support Group,
Selous Scouts,
P. Bag 3313,   12. 10. 1979
SALISBURY

<u>Attention: C/Sgt., Lewis</u>

Dear Sir,

Reference your letter regarding call up dates. My employer
and myself both feel that for me to do four months at one
stretch is the best policy, as it worked out well this year.

I feel that the best date would be from 1st February 1980 for
the duration of four months, if after this period I am
needed for an emergency call up, or similar circumstances, I
would only be too happy to oblige.

Yours faithfully,

Sgt., Hibbins G.S. 131283

Clearance Forms from Selous Scouts
upon transfer to the Chaplains Corp

CLEARANCE CERTIFICATE : SELOUS SCOUTS

No 131283   Rank: SGT.   Name HIBBINS G.S.

On being Posted/Discharged/Proceeding on leave (30 days or more)/Stood Down/
Proceeding on Course,

From : 24-1-80   (Date)   To : _____ (Date)

I understand that I must obtain all administrative clearance detailed below prior to my discharge being finalised, and should I fail to obtain such clearances, the authority for my discharge, resignation or retirement is automatically cancelled.

I am aware that it is an offence to wear items of military clothing with civilian dress without authority, and that if I am arrested for this offence I will be prosecuted.

Signature : _____

I, the undersigned hereby certify that the abovenamed is clear from any sub-unit/department/access/fund (as applicable) and has no outstanding debts other than those indicated in column (c).

Department and Detail	Date (b)	Debt (c)	Signature (d)
	29/1/80	NK	
...... CLOTH	30/1/80	NIL	
QM			
i. Vehicle Tools.	30/1/80	NIL	
			...(QM)
Trg Officer			
i. Pamphlets and Trg aids.	30/11/80	NIL	...(Trg OFF.)
QM			
i. ID Cards/passes returned.	29/1/80		
ii. Declaration — Official Secrets Act (on discharge or NTU only)			...(10)

a	b	c	d
RMO i. Medical (on discharge only)	29/1/80	Nil	*(signature)* (RMO)
RSO i. Scanlists. *(signature)* WRPL (CIPHERS) ii. Equipment. *(signature)*	29/1/80 29/1/80	NIL Nil	_____ (RSO)
Unit Accountant i. Mess Bill. ii. PRI Shop.	29.1.80 29.1.80	Nil NIL	M. Korpe *(signature)* _____ (Accountant)
Paymaster	29/1/80	Nil	*(signature)* (Paymaster)
Arms Storeman ie Unit Magazine/Armoury	29/1/80	Nil	*(signature)* (Storeman)
RSM	29/1/80	Nil	*(signature)* (RSM HQ)
RSM			_____ (RSM AB)
CSM (RS) HQ Cp	20/1/80	NIL	*(signature)* (CSM)
CSM (AB) HQ Cp	30/1/80	NIL	*(signature)* (CSM)

(OC/2ic HQ Gp)			*K.A.Rob* (OC/2ic HQ Gp)
GROUP Forwarding Address is : 26 ASCOT RD. AVONDECE, SBY		30/1/80	NIL *signature* (ORG/S)

signature
2ic

DISTRIBUTION
HS : Library P/F, 1 copy to member
2i : 1 copy only to T/S.

Testimonial from the Chaplain General

Telegrams: "RHODARMY" Salisbury
Telephone: 707451

Rhodesian Corps of Chaplains
ARMY HEADQUARTERS,
PRIVATE BAG 7720,
CAUSEWAY,
SALISBURY,
RHODESIA.

Reference.............................

..............................April 19 80

TO WHOM IT MAY CONCERN

I have known 131283 Sergeant Greg Hibbins since January 1980 when he joined the Rhodesian Corps of Chaplains.

Sergeant Hibbins has been a hardworking, determined and enthusiastic member of the Corps. During his service he proved to be capable and efficient, and was able to cope with his responsibilities in serving the Lord.

In his capacity as Chaplains Assistant, Sergeant Hibbins was an asset to his Corps, possessing a good sense of humour and who gained the respect of his fellow workers.

I have no hesitation in recommending him for any position which he may be offered.

(N. Wood) Lieutenant Colonel,
Chaplain General.

VAC/

Registration of Proof of Qualified Journeyman Status

THE INDUSTRIAL COUNCIL FOR THE MOTOR INDUSTRY

REGISTERED IN TERMS OF THE INDUSTRIAL CONCILIATION ACT (CHAPTER 267)

Certificate of Registration as a Journeyman

This is to Certify

that Gregory Stuart HIBBINS

has submitted satisfactory evidence to the Industrial Council for the Motor Industry that he has qualified as a Journeyman in the trade of Motor Mechanic's Work

in terms of the definition of journeyman contained in the Council's Agreement.

Given at Salisbury on the nineth day of September, 19 80, on behalf of

Appendix 2: Testimony Ring

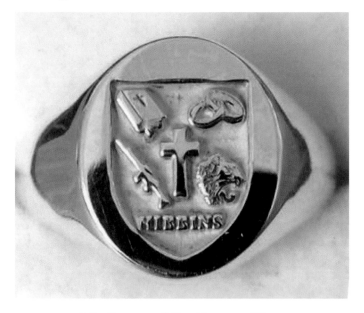

My Personal Testimony Ring

The Cross

The cross is central because of the sacrifice Christ made for me; my realisation of that was the defining moment in my life. I was raised in a home that practiced Spiritism, and from the age of nine was trained to be a medium. By the age of fifteen, I was a fully-fledged medium. My Dad died when I was fifteen; he was not into Spiritism.

Just after I turned sixteen, I came to know the Lord Jesus and was 'born again.' The fact that I had become a Christian was a huge problem for my mother; she issued me with an ultimatum! 'Lose Jesus or leave home!' I knew what Christ had done for me, so at the age of sixteen I left home and joined the Rhodesian army. Rhodesia was waging a bush war, and men were in short supply.

The Rifle

The rifle pictured is the FN-FAL 7.62, the rifle I used during my army days. From the tender age of three years old, my Dad taught me to shoot. For my fourth Christmas, my Dad gave me a Diana 27 .177 air rifle. Shooting has always been a passion of mine, and the discipline I learnt in those early years has been invaluable in my life. I experienced a huge amount during my army days, and I saw God's hand move many times. Towards the end of the Rhodesian bush war, I received a call from God to enter full time Christian ministry.

The Bible

God's Word has been transformational in my life; it has impacted every area. As an ordained minister, it is my 'lamp and light,' and it is the **absolute truth**. I have preached God's Word for more than 36 years, and daily I experience its power and comfort. In the current age of 'relative truth,' I have tried to preach the Word with integrity and without compromise. My motto is borrowed from that great South African evangelist, Roger Voke, who said "God said it, I believe it, and that settles it."

The Wedding Rings

Marriage is a creation ordinance, and my marriage to Glenys was the second most significant event in my life after my conversion to Christ. Glenys, and the fruit of our marriage, our children and grandchildren, have been my greatest blessing. My wife is a very special person who has helped me grow, both as a person and as a godly man. The wedding rings symbolise my never-ending love for her and our family.

The Lion

The lion symbolises a number of things. I have a lion personality type—very focused with a roar and a bite—but also a heart as soft as a marshmallow 😊. I am not scared to speak the truth in love, and I am most definitely not a politician. Also, I love the bush and have spent a significant amount of time in the African bush—and I love the lion most of all. I was privileged to serve for a number of years as an honourary game ranger in the world-renowned Kruger National Park, and my time there was precious. We lived on the border of the park and visited many hundreds of times.

So that is my testimony ring; what's yours?

www.greghibbinsbooks.uk

Printed in Great Britain
by Amazon